TELL ME A STORY

It's Life or Death...

JD Hamilton

JSJ Publishing

ISJ PUBLISHING

ISBN-13: 9798871885772
ISBN-10: 1477123456

Cover design by: JSJ Publishing
Printed in the United Kingdom

For Eddie. I promised you one day I'd write a book.
We're nearly there. I miss you every day.

CONTENTS

PREFACE

This was never meant to be my debut book.
After 25 years of reporting on true crime, writing fiction seemed like a pipe dream.
As a child my imagination was wild. If I wasn't reading a book I was writing stories.
But working full-time and being a mum took priority and for many years, my creativity disappeared into the darkest unreachable recesses of my mind.
Then I quit my job. I was burnt out. I needed a break from journalism.
I put pen to paper and began to write. And the words flowed.
The stories in this book were previously published

on my private blog - readers told me they liked them. And wanted more.
So, while I put the finishing touches to my first full-length novel, I thought I'd send this little collection out into the world. I hope you enjoy them.
The title comes from the words I used to say to my late, dearly-missed Gran, Anne, "tell me a story...".

PROLOGUE

"Death is not the opposite of life, but a part of it."

HARUKI MURAKAMI, CONTEMPORARY JAPANESE WRITER.

TELL ME A STORY

THE SUITCASE

I'd arranged to meet him in a coffee shop. They were always busy but big enough that any chatter was reduced to a hum in the background allowing you to have a conversation.

I spotted him immediately. Probably because among the groups of mums and toddlers, construction workers, office staff and students, he looked as if he'd just stepped out from the set of a 1950s movie and totally out of place.

He wore a brown two-piece wool suit, the collar on his shirt starched perfectly stiff, sharp crease down the trousers, light tan coloured tie knotted very thinly and perfect shoes you know he'd slowly,

proudly buffed and rubbed into a glossy shine. The little hair he had was slicked back with some gel and he sat with the confidence and poise only a man who had lived a lifetime could possess.
He gave a slight nod in greeting but his ox-eyed stare gave nothing away. At his feet was a tattered old suitcase. The kind they had in the 40s - worn brown leather stretched over an iron frame with brass caps. The brass handle had been rubbed with gold at one point but it had clearly been well used as the colour had mostly worn off. Unless he was planning to go on holiday after our meeting, it was an odd item to bring and I couldn't help wonder what was inside.

As I sat down across from him, he observed me, sizing me up. I had the feeling he'd got the measure of me before I'd even uttered 'hello'.
Finally, he spoke in a deep, gravelly voice that sounded like it had been crafted by years of whisky and cigarettes.
"You're probably wondering what's in the suitcase,"

he said, his eyes glinting with a hint of amusement.
I couldn't deny it. "Yes, I am," I replied, intrigued.
He leaned forward, his voice dropping to a whisper.
"It's a story," he said. "One that's been with me for a long time."
As he spoke, his hand went to his inside pocket and he hesitated for just a second, as if he was savouring the moment or perhaps still deciding what to tell me.
He brought out a stack of old papers, decaying with age, and bound together with twine. He handed them to me, and I could feel the weight of his story in my hands.
"It's a tale of love..."
He went silent again. I looked down at the yellowing papers and thought about what I was going to say next.
"Mr Millar," I cleared my throat. "I appreciate you wanting to tell me your story but I'm not a features writer. I'm a crime writer..."
I allowed my voice to sound puzzled because, quite

frankly, I was. My boss had taken the call this morning and ordered me to meet this old chap because he said he'd witnessed a terrible crime and wanted to talk to a reporter.

He didn't seem distressed, far from it, and I couldn't detect any urgency in his manner or tone that suggested the crime he had witnessed was recent.

My head was spinning with stress. I had a million things to do back at the office so being forced into coming here and meet with someone without any idea what they wanted to tell me was annoying to say the least.

I had deadlines and traipsing through Edinburgh city centre to sit in a coffee shop with a stranger who wanted to talk about his love life was not what I had signed up for.

Mr Millar's eyes narrowed as he took in my words. "A crime writer, you say?" he repeated, as if the concept was foreign to him.

I nodded, feeling a little uncomfortable. His tone had been almost mocking. "Yes, I specialise in

writing about murders, investigations, that sort of thing," I said, trying to sound confident.
He pursed his lips. "Well, that's a shame my story doesn’t seem to interest a crime reporter," he said finally. He rested his hands on the table as if he was going to use them as a spring to push himself up off the seat.
Maybe it was the hurt look in his eyes or the almost pathetic way he sat as if the weight of the world was on his shoulders but I started to feel like I was being too harsh. I softened a little. It wasn't his fault my working life was too busy.
"OK, I’d like to hear your story," I said, leaning forward.
Mr Millar smiled then, revealing a set of nicotine-stained teeth. "I thought you'd never ask," he said, and began to speak.

“She was the most beautiful girl in the room. Women, in my day, were naturally beautiful, a little bit of lipstick and some paint on their cheeks not like you see nowadays with their eyebrows tattooed on, clown faces with their make up painted on. My girl just glowed from the inside out. I'd just come home on leave during my national service," he paused and squinted his head. "You know what that is don't you?"

I nodded but said nothing. Part of my training as a journalist was let them speak, stay quiet, it makes people talk faster and tell you more to fill in the gaps. I've got to be honest though, his story was boring me already and my silence was just so he'd hurry up and get to the point.

He seemed happy to let me be quiet and seemed to drift off into another world as he spoke. "My friend had asked if I fancied going to the dancing. I'm not much of a dancer but I hadn't been around anyone other than men for so long that even just twirling some pretty girls round the dance floor seemed like a good idea to me. I wasn't looking for romance." He winked and I returned it with a smile. It didn't hurt to humour him, I thought.

"She was the first woman I noticed. I didn't have eyes for anyone else that night or since. She was a sassy little thing, my Jeannie. She was standing on the edge of the dance floor tapping her foot when I saw her."

He reached over and took the pile of papers from me and pulled out a photo. "Here she is," he said pointing to the yellowed paper in his other hand.

The photo was grainy black and white but clear enough to see. Jeannie Millar was a beauty no doubt about it. Brunette hair, I think, curled down to the tip of her shoulders, huge eyes and an expressive happy mouth. She was smiling and holding a bunch of flowers in her hand. She was wearing a knee-length skirt and blazer.

Mr Millar had been a very handsome young man. His hair was a curly mop on top which he'd smoothed down, the suit he had on looked very similar to the one he was wearing now. I actually glanced up to be sure it wasn't. He looked very happy. They were

clearly very much in love.
“That was our wedding day,” he said proudly.
“She waited for me to finish my service. We didn’t have much money. I got a job in a bottle factory and it wasn’t too bad money wise. Enough to rent us a wee house. We were very happy.” He closed his eyes and stayed like that for so long I wondered if he’d fallen asleep.
“Mr Millar?” I tried to keep the impatience out of my voice but failed miserably.
He chuckled. “Young people today. No patience, always in a hurry, heh."
He made a tapping motion on the table in front of him and continued with his story.
"We lived in a little bubble at first. Just the two of us. Jeannie had no desire to have a child. She said we had to have fun before we settled down into boring married life."
His face seemed to darken then, his eyes became even more hooded and I felt a little shiver go down my spine.

Almost immediately he brightened again and I wondered if I'd just imagined the coldness coming from him in those few seconds.

He suddenly thumped the table. Hard. I jumped.

"Goodness me, I am so rude. Would you like a cup of tea or one of those fancy coffees? You've been listening to me prattle on and must be thirsty? I know I am. How about a little cake too?"

"A coffee would be great. Just regular filter for me please." He stood up, ramrod straight, and bent down for his suitcase. Surely, he could leave it at the table for a few minutes, I thought, but no, he marched up to the counter, surprisingly spright considering he must be late 70s early 80s at least, suitcase in his hand. He ordered our drinks then disappeared to the gents.

When he came back, he seemed tired and drained.

He smiled at me but it didn't quite reach his eyes.

"Getting old means even talking for a while makes

you tired. Appreciate your youth and your energy while you can young lady. Time goes by fast."
I grimaced at the patronising statement but kept my tone light.
"Mr Millar, I appreciate you telling me your story but I really need to get back to the office. Do you think you could tell me what you think it is our, er, readers might be interested in?"
He raised one eyebrow and said: "My dear girl, I'd like to think your readers would appreciate the art of good story-telling. I don't think you'll have too much trouble selling my story.
"Now, where was I? Oh yes, Jeannie's refusal to have children. I was desperate to be a father but no matter how much I pleaded with her she was adamant that she wasn't having a child until she was at least 35. Which was quite old for a first baby in our time. She was wild. She loved to party and every spare moment we had was spent at parties or in the club. I was exhausted and saw another ten years of a social whirlwind before me.

"I felt quite cross with her but she won me round after a few days. She was such a gay girl. Always happy, always smiling especially if she had a drink in her hand, music in her ears and handsome men falling at her feet."

I felt a twinge of sympathy for him and glanced at their photo again.

Jeannie Miller wasn't classically beautiful but she had something about her that I could imagine had men eating out of her hand.

I realised he was still talking and tuned back in.

"Most nights I would come home from work and she wasn't home. She'd stumble through the door long after bedtime, drunk and giggling. She called me an old fuddy duddy and a bore. I loved her with every fibre of my being but her antics were destroying our marriage. I was miserable. I thought about divorcing her even if it meant a broken heart.

"However, I decided to give it one last shot. I begged her to come away with me on a little holiday. I'd seen some advertisements for a holiday caravan down by the sea in East Lothian.

"I thought we could have romantic walks on the beach, picnics, dinner by candlelight and I could talk to her properly away from all the influences in the city. I hoped she would listen."

He pointed to the suitcase.

"We didn't have a suitcase. I found this in a second hand shop. It was practically brand new."

I don't know if it was his age or because he was emotional but his eyes seemed a little wet. I could guess where the story was going and was still trying to work out why he thought a national newspaper would be interested. Maybe he just needed to talk to someone?

"Do you have any family, Mr Millar?" He shook his head.

"No, everyone is long dead. It's just me now." His voice was matter of fact. He wasn't looking for sympathy but I offered my condolences anyway.

He shrugged. "That's life isn't it. We all die. Some earlier than others." He said this very deadpan.

My coffee had gone cold but I took a sip anyway and glanced round the shop. The morning crowd had departed and the lunch crowd was sparse. Nobody could afford pre-packed sandwiches that cost just under a tenner. My tummy rumbled. I'd missed breakfast to come here and it looks like I was going to miss lunch too. I had to get him to get to the point or we'd still be here for dinner. My phone, which was on silent, had 20 missed calls. Probably my news desk wondering where the hell I was. I seethed at my boss. This was all his fault.

Mr Millar cleared his throat. I hadn't realised I'd drifted off into my own world. I sat up straighter. "My apologies, I was thinking about the office and my deadlines coming up...." I said pointedly.

He took the hint and pointed to the bundle of papers. "There's a newspaper in there that might interest you," he added.

I flicked through the yellowing papers and sure enough there was a folded piece of newspaper print. My paper! And it was a front page. I unfolded it carefully and looked at the splash. 'HUNT FOR WOMAN WHO FELL INTO THE SEA,' the headline screamed.

I read further down.

'The Coastguard are hunting for a married woman who fell into the North Sea while on holiday. Jean Millar was with her husband, Patrick, when she tripped on loose stones on the Old Cove Harbour in Cockburnspath, East Lothian.

'Her bereft husband has been keeping vigil on the pier and watching the search efforts since she disappeared three days ago.'

I stopped reading and looked up at him. I didn't need to read more to guess what had happened.

"They never did find Jeannie," he said. His voice was flat. Not so much raw grief but sadness. His eyes looked wet again.

"For over five days they searched the sea and tried to work out where her body would wash up but it never did. She disappeared the same day we were due to go back home. It had been a lovely week but she wanted to go back to Edinburgh earlier than I'd planned. She said she was bored with beach walking, the salt air was ruining her hair, she missed her friends."

He made a sound like a 'tut'. Irritation had replaced sadness.

I looked back down at the paper. There was a photo of Mr Millar. He was standing with his back to the photographer looking out to sea. I noticed what was sitting at his feet. I brought the paper closer and looked down at his feet again. The suitcase. I felt my heart just shatter for him.

"I'm very sorry about your wife, Mr Millar. I take it you contacted us because you want me to do an appeal?"

He stunned me when he suddenly laughed. It wasn't a soft giggle either, it was a full-on laugh that came from deep in his belly.

"My dear, you cannot seriously think I'm wanting an appeal in your paper to find the body of a woman who has been dead for 50 years? No, no, I'm sorry, you misunderstand me. I know exactly where my wife is. I've always known."

I was confused and it showed on my face.

He sighed. "I'm an old man, very old, my time is coming to an end. There's nobody left except me. I never met another woman who could equal her so there is no-one here to care about me but I need to tell someone before I shuffle off this mortal coil. A confession, if you like."

He moved the cups out of the way and hoisted the case onto the table. It was then I realised it was quite heavy. He stroked the soft leather....it was almost a caress.

"If only Jeannie had been more sensible. I didn't object to her shenanigans. All I wanted was a child, someone to love and love me back. A child would've calmed her down, brought some order to her day. Routine. But instead she craved drink, she craved attention from a bunch of uncouth roughnecks she would flirt with to get them to buy her alcohol. I was content to wait. I knew one day her looks would fade and the other men would drift off but she would be with me. The one man who truly adored her....I would have given her anything she desired."

His face twisted in anger. "It wasn't enough. She taunted me that last night we were together. She said she wished she'd never married me but she'd needed to get out of her home, her parents were stifling her and treated her like a child.

"Jeannie chose me because she knew I was a nice guy. Mild Mannered Patrick Millar. Mr Nobody. She thought she could keep me waiting meekly at home while she lived the life of a single woman.

"Jeannie threw it in my face that I would never be a father because she couldn't have children. She'd kept that a secret but was finally admitting it because she wanted to be free of me, to divorce me and never set eyes on me again. She said I bored her and made her feel sick whenever I touched her."

I leaned across the table and took his hand. "Mr Millar, did you push Jeannie into the sea?"

He blinked. "Don't be absurd!"

I felt like a fool. "Oh, I'm sorry...I didn't..."

He cut in, his eyes were as black as coal: "You should have asked if I killed her? Of course I did. But I didn't push her into the sea. That would have meant she'd have the freedom she craved, away from me."
He flicked the latches on the case and slowly opened the case. My eyes were drawn to the contents.....
"Oh no, my dear, she wasn't getting free of me that easily. You see, I carry her with me every single day....."

BABY OF MINE

Sophie sighed and closed her purse. 20p. That's all she's had. Her lower lip trembled as she contemplated the contents of her cupboard. Two tins of watery supermarket own brand baked beans, some spices and rice. She reached into the dark corner shelf of the expensive larder they'd installed when they were refitting the kitchen and her hand touched something. It was soft. Bread! 'Please be bread,' she muttered. She pulled it out - the dark green spots instantly visible. Tears welled up in her eyes. "For fuck sake!" It was about two weeks out of date. She wondered if she could cut out the mould and make shapes from the

rest. Would it make the children ill?
"Not as ill as they would be not having anything to eat for a week," she muttered, wiping angry tears from her eyes.
Her mother used to say "no use crying over spilt milk, just get on with it," which would be OK if she actually had any milk to cry over.
She didn't fancy black tea but beggars can't be choosers so she put the kettle on and went through the motions of making a cup of tea while she considered her options.
It wasn't always like this, Sophie thought.
Six months ago her life had been normal and happy. She lived with Brian, her husband, and their three children. It was a perfect life, she thought. Life had been good.
But Brian is gone now.
He died in a car crash on a very wet Wednesday night.
The police had knocked on her door and that was that. She'd been making spaghetti bolognese for tea

and thinking ahead to bath-time when they came to tell her.

In just a few seconds her life as she knew it was over. She hates the sound of a door being knocked. She calls it the death rattle.

Stricken with grief, Sophie found solace in the bottom of a vodka bottle, well actually, any bottle she could get her hands on. Friends who had rallied round her after the tragedy soon disappeared back to their own happy lives as if somehow by association the devastation that had befallen her might be contagious.

Her family tried but they too wearied of her rambling drunken cries and dishevelled appearance. She looked and felt like an old bag lady you see on American crime dramas wandering aimlessly with their shopping trolleys full of their worldly goods and mumbling about how fucked up their lives were. Her hair hadn't been washed in weeks or maybe it was months. She couldn't remember. Sophie shrugged. She'd been pretty at one time but sorrow and drink soon changed that. Her eyes were permanently red, from tears or vodka it was hard to tell. She didn't care.

She picked at a scab on her lip while she waited for the kettle to boil. They would be home from school soon. Maybe she could make rice and beans and tell them it was chilli?

She might get away with it with the two younger ones but Callan, her now 9-year-old was a smart cookie. He'd turn his nose up at it for sure, she thought. Sweet Jenny, the middle one at 5, would probably hate it but she was a kind girl and was too shy to speak her mind anyway. And her baby, precious little Carly, would chomp away quite happily on cardboard never mind beans and rice.

"What kind of a mother are you anyway? You need to get your act together. Brian isn't coming back. Ever." Dark thoughts threatened to creep in. She shook her head as if to shoo them away.

She heard a cry from upstairs. Nap time was over. She walked into the nursery. It was a beautiful room.

They'd decorated it pink when they knew they were having a girl.
It had been blue when she was pregnant with Callan. Brian had been so happy he was going to have a son. They did everything together. Brian did the school runs and the football practice and was there every Saturday morning cheering Callan on from the sidelines. He was a typical football dad. He dreamt Callan would be the new Pele or David Beckham.
Tears pricked at her eyes as she remembered her loving and handsome husband. He let Jenny put pink bows in his hair and lipstick on and she'd tell him he was "sooo pretty, daddy."
He had been devoted to them all. Brian hadn't been interested in anything but his family.
When she fell pregnant with Carly, their little surprise baby, they kept the nursery pink.
A smile crossed her face as she thought about the weekend trip to Glasgow that had resulted in baby number three but then her thoughts turned gloomy again when she realised that Brian only got to see

Carly for a few weeks before his car slid on black ice and ploughed into the path of an oncoming gritter lorry. It would be funny if it wasn't so tragic.

The baby's cries grew louder as if in protest at how long she was taking. She approached the cot and smiled at her daughter whose little eyes twinkled so blue you would swear you were looking into the sea.

"Mummy's here baba." She scooped up the baby and made her way back to the kitchen.

"Your brother and sister will be home soon from school. We should get you dressed. You are so pretty my little angel." She made kissing sounds as she nuzzled her face against her baby's soft skin. She heard Carly laugh - the delicious musical sound only babies can make.

Sophie gently washed and dressed her baby, cooing as she went, trying to stem the bubble of anxiety that was gurgling away in her throat. How was she going to feed her children? " They're going to take my children from me."

Panic gripped her. She can't lose her children as well.

She shook her head as if to clear her mind from such thoughts.
She sat with Carly on her knee and began to sing "Baby mine, don't you cry. Baby mine, dry your eyes. Rest your head close to my heart, Never to part, baby of mine."
She was aware as she sang of a shadow crossing over her. She squeezed her eyes shut. 'Not yet, not yet. I'm having a moment with my baby,' her mind screamed.
"Sophie? Sophie…" the voice was gentle.
"Carly woke up. She's hungry. I dressed her and we were just singing but now she needs fed."
"OK Sophie, why don't I take Carly and you go have a little nap?"
"But Callan and Jenny will be home soon and I don't have any money and my cupboards are bare."
The face looking down at her frowned then smiled. "Don't you worry about that, my darlin', I'll sort out Callan and Jenny. Let's get you upstairs for a little while. You look exhausted."

"Babies are exhausting. I'm so tired." She stood up and gave Carly a kiss before handing her over. "Mummy will be back soon baba."

She allowed herself to be guided up the stairs. "I'll just close my eyes for a little while until the children are home."

She was fast asleep as soon as her head hit the pillow.

"She'll be out for a while," the woman turned to her companion.

She handed Carly over. "Make sure that doll is back in the cot for when she wakes up."

"This feels wrong. Surely she knows it's not a real baby? Why are we allowing her to think her children are still alive? This isn't helping her. She needs to accept all of them died in the crash. She needs to grieve and move on."

"She's not ready yet. She needs the doll and she needs to believe that Callan and Jenny are at school right now. You know the drill."

They closed the bedroom door and went downstairs. A moment later, Sophie's eyes flew open. She could hear Carly crying.

"My baby needs me…" She stood up. "Mummy's coming, baby, mummy's coming."

SWEET DREAMS

"When I grow up, Daddy, I'm going to get a good job and have lots of money and you'll never have to go to work again!" Catherine Evans wrapped her chubby little arms around Tommy's legs and squeezed the tears out. He sighed, bent down, feeling every bit of his 40 years as his back creaked in protest at the movement, and lifted his 6-year-old daughter into his arms. Her green eyes were flecked with defiance as she pursed her lips at the next few words she knew were coming.

"Catherine, my little sunshine, you know Daddy has to work. How else are we going to eat?"

"But it's Saturday and I want to go to the park, Daddy. You promised!"
Tommy Evans felt the weight of guilt bearing down on him. It was indeed the weekend and usually he made sure he could spend some time with his daughter but the rent had gone up again and Catherine needed new shoes. Since his wife had walked out it was just the two of them. The social work people had tried to get him to put Catherine in a home or with foster parents "because men don't look after their children in 1962!" but he loved his daughter and he wasn't like other men. He'd fathered her and she was his responsibility. He was lucky where they lived. The neighbourhood women looked out for Catherine when she came home from school and sometimes they'd give her a biscuit while she waited for him to finish work. Life was hard and money was scarce but they had a roof over their heads and food in their bellies. He'd never been one to spend an evening in the boozer like many of his peers. Their nights were dinner,

bath time and bedtime stories and their weekends were for trips to the park and sometimes if he had a bit money spare they'd take a wander round the zoo. His daughter didn't mention her mum...why would she? She'd scarpered as soon as Catherine turned six months so the kid didn't know any better. He loved his daughter fiercely and dreamed of giving her a better life than he'd had. She'd make something of herself, of that he was sure. The name Catherine Evans would be known forever. He could feel it in his bones.

"You can go to the park by yourself Catherine Evans. Now stop that snivelling and let Daddy go or else I'll be late and then what kind of trouble will we be in? You don't want me getting sacked do you?" He gave her hair a little ruffle and set her down. "Off you go now, child, and no more of this crying nonsense. You just stick in at school and maybe one day you can take care of your old dad but until then I'm off to earn a shilling." He softened his tone and smiled at her. "Who else is going to keep you in chocolate,

Katy girl?"

"C'mon Katy girl, just try it. It makes you feel brand new!" Catherine lifted her head. Nobody called her 'Katy girl' anymore. Her dad used to when she was little. But he'd got himself killed in a work accident when she was 6 and she'd been shunted off to a children's home. There followed a succession of foster homes where the women were cold hard bitches and the men had wandering hands particularly when she reached her teens and at times it was easier just to let them have their sneaky gropes if it meant they'd lob her an extra penny or two. A couple of times they were caught and she'd find herself back in the home and sharing a dorm with 30 other brats nobody cared about. At 16 she'd legged it and no-one had come looking. She'd married the first boy who'd taken an interest in her. Four kids later he had disappeared with his fancy woman and Catherine was left holding the babies.

Her cleaning job in the local pub kept the wolf from the door and her sanity intact.
"Katy! For fuck sakes man, where did you go?" She snapped out of her musing and blinked as her friend, Suzy, held out the joint and gestured for her to take it.
"Suze, I can't! What if one of the kids wake up and I'm stoned out my face?"
Suzy, who had five kids and no man, laughed like a drain. "You're not going to get stoned on one joint you fucking wimp. It's just to relax you. I do it all the time. Fuck knows we need something to escape this fucking shithole life." She took another drag and her pupils seemed to take on a life of their own. "Your eyes look like a kaleidoscope," Catherine laughed. Suzy, mellower than Catherine had ever seen her, gave a smile and a half shoulder shrug. "Sweet dreams are made of this.."she warbled.
Catherine took a huge gulp of vodka and coke, "OK, gimme it…"she held out her hand. Suzy winked, "attagirl," and handed the spliff to her friend.

"How you doing tonight, Katy?" Catherine was bent over fiddling with the strap on her sandal. Recognising the voice, she straightened her body upright and tried to fix her eyes on his face. She remembered he was one of the nicer coppers who didn't treat the street girls like a rancid stench that offended their nostrils. She tried to be nice but she was strung out and needed a hit and he was getting in her way.

"I'm awright." "Business slow tonight?" Catherine grimaced. "Well, aye and you two being here doesn't help." The cop, who looked like he should still be in school, shook his head. His name came to the surface of her mind but before she could catch the memory, it disappeared again. "It's a cold one tonight. Maybe take the hint the punters are staying in and get home to your kids?" "Are you telling me to move on, officer?" Her voice had an edge to it. Katy Evans had been a street girl for a while now.

She was 38 but looked 58 - she'd been a fine looking woman at one time but drugs, heroin, had ravaged her body and she was near skeletal. She'd always had a strong character, but the dependency on heroin had brought on a state of permanent anger and aggression. He treated her with kid gloves. He didn't want her kicking off because his partner, who hated prostitutes, would lift her. He knew there were four kids waiting for her at home. How they hadn't been removed by the social was beyond him. "I'm not telling you to move on Katy but it's almost midnight." He kept his tone light and calm. She responded by biting one finger nail and spitting it out at his partner's feet. She lifted her hand in a wave. "Am away hame then."

"Pete, this is really creepy down here. I don't like it. Can you take me home?" "We're in the car, Shell. Don't be a scaredy cat. C'mon, give me a cuddle. I'll protect you." He pulled her towards him and she snuggled her face into his shoulder. She could hear his breathing quicken and knew he wasn't planning on taking her home anytime soon. Not until he got what he came for. She pulled away and looked out into the darkness. The car park was a favoured spot for courting couples and other creatures of the night. Namely drug addicts, alcoholics and prostitutes who brought their clients down to the deserted spot to do their deeds. It was in the middle of nowhere and it was as dark as it was eerie. She shivered. The place gave her the chills. Suddenly she heard shouting and the slamming of a car door nearby. She squinted her eyes to see better and could just about make out the figure of someone standing by a car to their left. The headlights went off and it was pitch black again. A moment later the exhaust backfired and she heard the car roaring off. "Fucking hell Pete. I want to go home." "Fuck sake, Shell, it's just some couple having a barney and they've fucked off." "Someone got out of the car and they're probably skulking around watching. It's giving me the creeps." Pete knew he wasn't getting his way with Michelle until he'd shown her they were alone down here. He got out of the car. Michelle also got out. "I'm not staying in the car by myself." "Fucking women," he muttered. They walked about 500 yards towards the direction of the car they'd seen. Michelle was clinging to his arm and jumping at every little sound. "Look, there's nothing or nobody here. Just a bag of dumped rubbish," he pointed to the heap on the ground. Michelle sighed with relief and turned back towards their car but just as she did something glinted in the moonlight. A silver button. She turned back around and gingerly moved forward, pulling Pete's arm with her. Her piercing scream shattered the night air and sent Pete stumbling back onto his arse. "It's a body!" She screamed the words over and over.

Bert McGuire was pissed off. He'd been woken from

a very nice whisky induced sleep to come look at a hooker's body found in the middle of the fucking countryside. Nobody had told him how she'd died so he was guessing she'd had a bit too much of the funny stuff. "Who the fuck decided a street tart overdosing was worth disturbing my sleep?" He shouted to no-one in particular. The other cops assembled at the scene turned away feigning ignorance. The Chief Inspector could be a right bastard when he was in a mood. McGuire homed in on one poor Police Constable. "You! What in God's name do you think I can do with this at 3 in the fucking morning? Have the van come collect her and she can go to the mortuary. Someone will know who she is." The young PC was about to nod when a brave Detective Sergeant cleared his throat and said: "Boss, er, we think it's murder, sir." McGuire went red in the face. "Who made you Columbo you fucking bellend." He swept his arm around the scene. "Can you see a fucking thing in this darkness?" He bellowed. The DS, maybe he was on a death wish that night, squared his shoulders. "I don't think we should move her sir. Not until the pathologist has had a look. She's got some nasty injuries.Sir." The cops at the scene didn't think it was possible for Bert McGuire's fleshy scarlet face to go even redder but it seemed to take on a new hue of a postbox colour with incandescent rage. McGuire opened his mouth to scream obscenities at the DS when a voice stopped him in his tracks.

"Chief Inspector McGuire! Why hasn't this scene been secured? God sakes man, are you still drunk?" McGuire's heart sank. His boss, the Chief Superintendent, was a right bloody do-gooder. No way was he getting back home to his scratcher tonight.

Chief Superintendent Malcolm Cassidy had risen through the ranks the hard way. A natural leader with the heart of a beat bobby he cared about his little patch and the citizens in it. McGuire was a thorn in his side he'd love to see booted off the force. "This woman, a prostitute or not, deserves the same care and attention you would give to anyone else who has died in suspicious circumstances. Seal off this area and secure her remains. The pathologist is on his way. Where are the people who found her?" McGuire could only give a hapless shrug of his shoulders as another constable stepped forward. "Excuse me sir. PC Steven Douglas sir. I, er, I know this woman." Cassidy raised an eyebrow. The PC stammered. "Not in that way, sir. I would see her on my beat most nights. She's been a street worker for a few years. A drug addict. Mum of four young children. She, er, was a bit on the feisty side and would argue with her punters a lot. She wasn't always like that but the drugs took hold sir and she did this work to pay for her drugs. She's most likely had a fight with one. Her name is Catherine Evans."

Steven Douglas was downcast. Maybe it was because he was getting older but he found himself surrounded by ghosts. He was haunted by cases -

the victims and their killers. Especially the ones that got away. 29 years a police officer and of course there's a few who 'got away'. A serial killer. A rapist. Dozens of annoying bloody housebreakers. And more than a few murderers. He was seeing the faces of the victims over and over. They were haunting his dreams. One more so than the others. Catherine Evans. She'd died just an hour after he'd spoken to her. Was it guilt? Had he done the wrong thing that night not letting his partner arrest her? Sure, she'd have spent the night in the cells but that would have been better than spending an eternity in a bloody grave. He thought about her often. Back when he was a PC he'd sometimes dug out the case file and harassed the CID to look at it again. But they were overrun with cases and a murdered prostitute in the 1980s wasn't high on their list of priorities so they'd make the right noises and say they'd look at it when they got a minute but that minute never arrived. When he made the CID himself he would sometimes look at it in his own time. But it was a dead end. No other women had been murdered in the same way, there wasn't any forensics they could get from her body and the witnesses were non-existent. Anyone who might have been hiding in the woods surrounding the car park had never come forward. But Catherine deserved justice. He got up and looked out the window. A ruler surveying his kingdom. What else could he do for Catherine? For her children who deserved to see the bastard who'd stabbed her over and over and then left her mutilated body like a pile of discarded rubbish in court and punished for his crime.

"Laura? It's Chief Constable Steven Douglas. I wonder if you would do me a favour? Yes, it's a story for you. A cold case. 25 years ago this month. I'm putting a new team on it and reopening it. Can you write this in the paper? A killer got away with it but I want the people of this town to know we never forget a case especially not the murder of a young mother."

"Mr Douglas. It's DCI Andrew Banks from the police Cold Case Unit. My boss thought you might want to know we have a DNA profile on the Catherine Evans murder. I know you spent many years on this case and have spoken about it since you retired sir so we thought this is a development you'd be interested in. The profile isn't on the DNA database which means her killer isn't known to us but we are plugging away on it, Sir. Even 35 years down the line."

Catherine saw the car come towards her. She turned to make sure the coppers were gone. She quite liked the younger officer. PC Douglas! That was his name! He had a kind face. He'd go far that one, she thought. His mate was a wrong 'un though. She'd heard the other girls talk about him and his cruelty towards them. She was feeling shivery. Hopefully this punter was just after a quickie then she could go meet her dealer and feel all warm and good about herself again. She didn't recognise the car. A newbie, she thought. None of the other girls were around. It was a cold, wild night and they'd all disappeared. This one was hers. He stopped beside her and she got in.

He took her to a deserted carpark far out of town. Somewhere in her drug addled brain she thought he's not a newbie at all. He knows this is where the hookers come to do business. He wasn't much of a talker either which suited her. She stared out the window, sighed and then put on her brightest smile and said: "Ok then darlin', money first then lets get down to it." He turned to her. "I'm not paying for it, you slag! You'll give me a freebie." He grabbed her arm, his face twisted in anger. Catherine let out a yelp but her own temper kicked in. She was desperate for some junk and this fucker had just wasted her time. She punched him square in the face with all the fury a 5ft 5" woman could muster. All her pent-up rage and disappointment was clenched in that fist. "Fuck you, you cheap bastard!" While he was writhing around in his seat, the pain from her daddy's signet ring stinging his eye, she grabbed her handbag and dived out the car. Incensed she stood in front of his vehicle and screamed obscenities at him. She was so engulfed with anger she didn't see him until he was beside her. Something silver flashed by her eyes. She felt the first punch, then the second and third. She lost count by 5 as he stood over her thrusting the knife again and again. Moments later he jumped in his car and left her to die.As she floated on the edge of the abyss, Catherine Evan's mind took her to happier times. She was laughing as her daddy pushed her on a swing. "Higher, Daddy. I want to fly high!" She felt herself floating. "You're the best daddy ever. I'm glad you don't have to work anymore. I'm here now, Daddy."

WIRED FOR SOUND

Darkness terrifies her. She can't see anything. Not even her hand in front of her face.

She imagines this is what it is like in a coffin. A blackness that cocoons your body. Is death just a black void filled with…nothing?

She wasn't born for noise. Silence doesn't worry her. The quiet is soothing and comforting. Noise gives her a headache. But when the lights go out her imagination betrays her.

Was that thump she thinks she heard a remembered

sound from long ago? There's a vibration from the attic. Is someone up there? Just waiting. Is there, right at this minute, someone breathing in the corner of the room, watching her?

She tries to recall what the sound of breathing is like. A rasp? A throaty, scratching sound? Or a peaceful hum? Dammit, she can't remember.

Are they waiting until sleep overtakes her and she's vulnerable. She strains her eyes and summons every ounce of cognitive ability she can, willing her ears to carry sound to her brain so she can distinguish if it's her imagination or someone really has crept into her bedroom in the dead of night.

She bolts upright and somehow in her sleep-filled state she knows she is alone. There's nothing there. There never is. Go back to sleep. She sleeps fitfully. Her brain never stops. It's wired, listening for the sounds she will never hear.

Her brain remembers some sounds from long before her ears failed her and can reassure her.

The soft whistle of white noise she hears in the

daylight has been replaced by the stillness of night, there's the rustling of a scavenging fox, the pitter patter of raindrops on the window that she can see and imagine but not hear, a howling wind clattering against the front door, the squeak of the floorboard on the third step from the top that she's been meaning to fix for years.

She settles back into a slumber, praying for one night of uninterrupted sleep.

There it is. The creak as someone stands on the old floorboard. She jumps up, heart hammering. Someone IS here. She squeezes her eyes shut as if this will somehow offer her protection.

You idiot. As if that's going to help. Her eyes fly open. The handle is being pushed down slowly. It stops again. Has he changed his mind? Fear has her rooted to the spot. She's clutching the duvet under her chin. This is it, she thinks, all the years of being scared of the dark, scared the bogeyman was coming and here he is.

Was she psychic? Did she foresee her grisly, violent

end? Is that why she's been scared of everything, scared of living, scared of dying, for as long as she can remember?

Her brain is firing off in a million directions at the speed of lightning. There's nowhere to run. By the time she's got the window open he will be beside her. She reaches across to her side and desperately searches for a weapon, anything to stall the inevitable.

Her clammy hand touches something. A book. No good. The remote control for the television? Why, oh why, didn't she slip something more helpful into her bedside drawer. Like a knife. Or a hammer. A baseball bat. You are so stupid. There's no chance to say goodbye to anyone. I was mean to my mum today. I said a horrible thing to my brother. I was rude to the shop assistant. I didn't eat the chocolate bar I was saving as a treat. My new skirt will never be worn. You really are a fucking idiot. Saving for best. Why? Now you're not going to see 'best' because the monster is coming. What a great epitaph - here lies the idiot saving things for best and who was a total bitch to everyone on her last day.

Isn't it fitting the wind is howling? The hour of my death and it's pitching a fucking storm outside. It's not even Halloween. Does he look like Michael Myers or is he a normal looking 'monster'. What does the last face I'm ever going to see look like? I hope he makes it quick. Fuck you, I'm not going quietly. She opens her mouth to scream when the door flies open.

All she can see is darkness from the hallway. Confusion muddles her brain. There's no-one there. Did she imagine the noises? Was she dreaming?

The black and white figure jumps onto the bed. Eddie! You stupid cat! You scared the life out of me. Why can't you meow louder? I can't hear you, why don't you understand that? She relaxes a little as she settles back down and tenderly rubs the space between his ears. Her heart rate is returning to normal. Her brain is relaxing again for just a second. She feels him purring beneath her hands. Her eyes close. Before long she's lost in a dreamless sleep. Until her brain hears the next sound.

EVERMORE

"You will never amount to anything! You're just like your mother! A useless good for nothing tart!" Jenny slammed her bedroom door shut before he'd finished shouting at her, but she could still hear him ranting and raving downstairs.

The crash of broken glass, the thud of something being thrown against the wall. At least he was confining his rage to objects and not her. She threw herself down onto her bed and curled up into a ball, tears streaming.

She forced her fist into her mouth to stop the screams welling inside her from bursting out. It was always the same. He'd come home from the pub drunk and menacing.

She did everything she could to placate him - food on the table, cold beer in the fridge - but if the urge took him, he would erupt about his "bitch" of a wife who had run away and left him with a "useless sponging" daughter.

Sometimes he'd grab Jenny by the throat and scowl at her before letting her go.

"You're not worth the beating. Get out of my sight and stay out."

He'd hit once or twice but not hard enough to leave any marks. He still wanted people to think he was a good dad.

Jenny thought that one day he might kill her. That drink and seething rage and the fact she had the misfortune to look like her mother would propel him to snuff her life out.

She stared up at the ceiling as silent tears fell.

"Maybe he'd be doing me a favour," she thought.

Jenny didn't have anyone else except her dad.

Her mum's family were too wrapped up in their own lives to care about what was happening to Jenny. Maybe it was embarrassment at their neglect. Jenny probably reminded them of their failures and shortcomings as siblings and adults. Out of sight, out of mind.

Her grandparents on both sides were long dead and buried. Her dad was an only child.

I am, thought Jennifer Evans, on my own.

I am an orphan.

It wasn't always like that. She supposed at one time her parents must have been happy and she had been borne from a loving relationship, not an illicit fumble in the dark.

Okay, she was an accident but at least she'd been wanted once they got over the shock.

That is, until the stress of a demanding baby, a house to keep and a husband who worked 15 hours a day became too much, and Jenny's mum just upped and left one day when Jenny was three.

Her dad came home to a home alone crying toddler

and a note that simply said: 'I can't do this.'
Her mum hasn't been seen since.
Jenny heard one of the aunts tell dad, mum was seen down south with a bloke but he got so angry that it seemed safer to just pretend mum is dead and not talk about her. So nobody mentioned her.
She might as well be anyway. Jenny can't really remember what she looks like, but she's told by everyone she looks like her. All blond hair and teeth. Jenny hates her mum. She hates her dad too but at least he hasn't abandoned her. Yet.

"Jenny!" Cheryl squealed in shock, but she was laughing.
"If your dad sees you dressed like that!" Cheryl was Jenny's only friend.
Other children at school mocked Jenny.
They called her horrible names, she wasn't fashionable, she didn't have any money for records or concerts, and she wore glasses that were too big

for her tiny face. She didn't have a mum.

She would see them whispering about her in their friendship groups and the girls would egg on the boys to be cruel.

But Cheryl, whose parents had been married forever and treated their daughters like princesses, was kind and popular and she'd decided Jenny was her best friend.

They'd met in class at the age of 7 and they'd been inseparable ever since.

Cheryl was Jenny's escape. Cheryl said Jenny was her evermore.

In Cheryl's house, Jenny could be a child. She enjoyed the light-hearted family dinners even if Cheryl's dad was a bit gruff and grumpy. Cheryl said it was just an act and his "bark was worse than his bite".

She could loll about the floor with Cheryl and watch television without being fearful of a shoe being levelled at her head or worse, an ashtray. They could play music and dance and laugh and nobody shouted or raised their hands in anger.

Jenny wished Cheryl's mum was hers.
Jenny giggled. 'What?" It was a rhetorical question said with a cheeky tone.
She turned to the mirror and applied thick blue eyeliner. "I'm just copying Madonna," she said.
She shrugged. "Anyway, it's Friday. Dad will be in the pub all weekend and I'll not see him until Sunday night."
Cheryl stood up. "Mum bought us these to wear to the disco tonight." She held up two skirts.
Jenny squealed in delight. 'A ra-ra skirt! I've wanted one of those for ages!" She grabbed the red and gold flounced material and held it against her body.
Cheryl laughed along. "We will look like twins. Mum got us tops to match and we can wear our leggings and ballet shoes. I've got a bag you can borrow."
Jenny wanted to weep with joy and sadness at her friend's kindness.
She hugged the skirt to her. "Maybe tonight Andy will notice me!" She sighed wistfully. Cheryl frowned: "Jen, he's a waste of space. You know Mikey

really likes you. And while we're talking about boys, no glasses tonight!" She whipped them off Jenny's face and threw them across the bedroom.

"I can't go out without my glasses, I'm nearly blind!"

Cheryl giggled: "I'll hold your hand all night."

Jenny made a prayer sign. "Maybe tonight I will get my first kiss."

They danced around the room singing 'Like A Virgin'.

"C'mon Jenny, just let me do it." He was heavy breathing in her ear, she could smell the cheap cider he'd drunk, and it was making her feel nauseous.

She pushed him away. "No, Andy.... we can't!"

Jenny was freezing. Andy had dragged her outside the youth club building and round the back. It was a cold night, and she didn't have a jacket.

He pulled her back towards him. "Oh, come on you know you want to."

His voice had gone whiny, and Jenny immediately

wondered what she'd ever seen in him.

He was sticking his tongue in her ear, and it was freaking her out. She felt all wet and slimy.

His other hand was slithering down her leg like a snake before grabbing her private parts and pinching roughly. This was not what she imagined in her daydreams. Her year-long crush vanished in a wave of repulsion and fury.

"Get off me!" He was too busy licking her face and fondling down below to pay attention to her words so she mustered up all the strength she could and pushed him firmly away.

He jumped back in shock at her rude interruption.

"You're disgusting Andy Scott! I'm only 14 and you're 18," she spat.

She was wiping her face trying to get his saliva smears off.

His face contorted in fury and his lips, lips she had dreamed of kissing for so long, grew thin and mean.

She shrank back against the wall.

"Disgusting, am I?" He grabbed her by the arm and

put his other hand around her throat. "I wasn't disgusting when you were flaunting yourself just begging for me to notice you."
He squeezed tighter as she tried to push him off with her free hand, but he was bigger and stronger, and he managed to get both her hands around her back. His lips were all over her face and he ran his tongue down her cheek.
"Don't fight it, you asked for this," he said.

Books became her escape. Whenever dad remembered to give her some money, she would run to the charity shop and hoover up the shelves. She read anything and everything.
Cheryl called her a bookworm and a bore.
Jenny didn't want to go to the youth club anymore. She rarely came out of her house. Cheryl's mum noticed Jenny didn't come around for tea as often, but Cheryl couldn't give her an answer why.
She took to hiding in the school library so Cheryl and

her friends couldn't find her. Jenny just wanted to be on her own.

Cheryl grew tired of trying to encourage her friend to join in.

Jenny was ashamed. She couldn't tell Cheryl what happened that night or why she had retreated and become a loner.

And so their friendship was abandoned. Jenny wrote in her diary: 'I miss Cheryl, but I can never tell her what Andy did to me, I would die from embarrassment. She might think I should've just let him anyway. I am OK on my own, I don't need anyone, I have my books and I have something nobody can take away from me - my imagination. One day I will be a famous writer and Mum will be begging me for forgiveness. Dad won't care, he's always too drunk to care about anything. But when Mum wants to come back into my life, I will tell her the same thing she said, 'I can't do this' and that will show her!"

"Jen? Hello!" Jenny was startled out of her daydream by the clicking of fingers in her face. "Wake up dozy. A few of us are going to the pub for some lunch. Do you fancy coming?" Jenny pushed back her chair and stood up, stretching the kinks out of her back.

She'd been sitting at the desk for hours.

"No, I've got to get this essay done. It's due in next week and I'm nowhere near finished." Her companion shrugged. "Your loss. Teacher's pet. I'll bring you back a doggy bag."

She gave him a playful punch on the arm.

"Away you go, some of us just want to graduate and not be layabouts all our lives."

She gave an exaggerated bow as she walked away, her mind already on crossing the finishing line with her essay and getting home before Dad staggered in from the pub.

Their relationship has changed slightly in the last ten years.

The shy timid teen had been steadily replaced by a resilient self-sufficient young woman.

She still shared a house with him, mainly due to finances, but they kept a distance from each other. Occasionally he would speak to her but mostly he just railed at the Gods when he was three sheets to the wind which was often.
He'd taken to spending huge amounts of time in the concrete jungle they called a garden. She'd come home late at night, and he'd be just sitting there.
It was strange but she didn't want to ask him why. She'd long given up trying to understand him.
On days when she was feeling particularly vengeful, she hoped he'd freeze to death but on other days, she thought she would feel nothing but sadness for the loss of her only parent. He was still there physically but he had long ceased to be 'dad'.
She'd read in a book it was called 'ambiguous grief' and she thought it was the perfect explanation for both her parents.
Dad hadn't abandoned her physically like Mum, but he might as well have done for all the good he'd been. Maybe she was more like her parents than she

thought. After all she'd skipped out on her relationship with Cheryl after Andy attacked her.
A deserter just like mum and dad.
She sighed: "the apple truly doesn't fall far from the tree," she thought.
Dad was sitting in the garden when Jenny got home. She was surprised. Usually, he was in the pub.
The house was in darkness. She walked into the kitchen and turned on the little light above the cooker to be able to see.
"Jenny..." He was standing at the back door. His tone was quiet, subdued even.
She turned around and looked at him.
He was still a healthy man in his 50s, but tonight he looked old and frail. As if he were carrying the weight of the world.
His back was slightly hunched. He looked miserable and sad, rather than angry.
Jenny didn't speak. She felt a bubble of laughter at the base of her throat.
Something about the way he was looking at her was

making her nervous for the first time in years. She pushed herself into the cooker and maintained eye contact.

"Come into the garden. I need to talk to you." He said

She raised her chin and pursed her lips. "It's freezing, dad. We can talk in here."

He shook his head and gripped onto the handle of the back door, half turning to go back outside. "Come outside, it's time to tell you the truth." He walked out.

"The truth? About what?" Almost involuntarily she walked towards him. "What are you talking about dad?"

He cleared his throat, and she was puzzled. He seemed very nervous which set her on edge. Sober Dad was just quiet and moody, drunk dad was loud and menacing. She'd never seen him edgy or tense like this.

"You look like her, you know."

"Who?"

"Your mother. You wear your hair the same way.

Pulled back tight like that in a ponytail. She was a beauty in her younger days."

"Why are you talking about her?"

"Because it's time. You're a grown woman now. You don't need mollycoddled anymore."

"You've never mollycoddled me."

"I gave you backbone, child. Courage. The ability to stand on your own two feet. I didn't have time to pet you."

"Pet me? I was 3 years old when she left! I was a child not an animal for God's sake!"

"You were fed and watered and given shelter. What more did you need?"

"Love? Affection maybe? Mum disappeared and you did too dad!"

"Love is for idiots! Love gets you nothing but misery. You should know that by now. There's no such thing as a happy ending Jenny."

"What's going on, Dad? It's bloody cold out here. I'm going back in."

"Don't you want to say hello to your mother?"

"What are you talking about? Has she been here? Today? Is this what's wrong?"
"She's here now, Jenny."
"Dad?" It came out like a croak.
"You see, child, she never left. She's over there."
Dad pointed to a spot in the garden that had been used as a dumping ground for all sorts of rubbish over the years. Waste from the front garden, old furniture, mattresses, bags of junk.
She was confused. There was nobody there. She looked over towards him and realisation dawned.
Jenny recoiled in shock.
She believed him.
A memory slammed into her mind.
Dad digging away in the garden, laying slabs over all of the grass.
She'd been upset because he'd smashed up all the furniture and her garden toys that same day.
Jenny thought she was going to be sick. Her stomach roiled and she felt like she was on a boat that was churning up every wave as it sailed along.

She sank onto the deckchair beside him. Tiny beads of sweat had broken out across her face.

Vomit swirled at the back of her throat. She swallowed it back down. Her heart was hammering. She wanted to scream.

His voice penetrated the silence.

"She wanted to leave me. She'd met someone else. Some good for nothing wastrel. She was going to take you with her."

"You murdered her."

"I saved her from making a mistake."

"She didn't abandon me. You took her!"

"Your mother had no right to make a decision like that! She wouldn't have coped with you, Jenny. She wanted to tear our family apart. I couldn't allow that."

"All these years I've hated her for leaving, the absolute hell of living with you alone. You destroyed all our lives. Why?"

"We were a family."

"Pfft, family?! You wouldn't know the meaning of

the word! Your wife wanted to leave you and you killed her. You beat me, you terrorised me! That's not how a father should be! Was it you who wrote the note?"

"No. I made her write it. You reminded me of her every day, that was my punishment. A cross I had to bear."

"You couldn't live with your guilt so you abused me. Why are you telling me this now, dad? Why?"

"I told you. It's time."

"Time for what?"

"To be a family again. All of us. Together."

In an instant he was beside Jenny, lifting her from the chair. A moment ago, he had seemed like a fragile old man but now he had a strength that had belied his physique. She was spun round so he was behind her, holding both her arms against her back, his own body was tight against hers.

She was transported back ten years to a moment in time when another man had held her against her will. This wasn't happening! Not again!

Instinctively, Jenny let out a scream as she gathered every ounce of strength she had in her body and twisted fiercely to free one arm. She swung it round and caught his head. The shock of her retaliation caused him to let go and Jenny cracked him across the face with her fist. He staggered back and she launched into a kicking frenzy, screaming as loud as she could.

Dad was on the ground, and she kept kicking and screaming.

She only stopped when someone pulled her off him.

The house was empty. All that was left to do was lock the front door and be on her way. Jenny wasn't sure what would happen to the house now. She didn't imagine anyone would want to live there knowing a body had lain in the garden for twenty years.

That a woman had met a violent end inside her own home.

Jenny had buried her mum properly. She would get a headstone when she could afford it but at least mum was in her final resting place and had some dignity. He'd discarded her like she was rubbish. Jenny wiped away a tear.

All she'd done for weeks was cry.

'Now, I really am an orphan,' she thought, 'and I've never felt so alone.'

"Jenny…" She turned her head in the direction of the voice. It was Cheryl standing with arms wide open and a huge smile on her face. Jenny let out a sob and ran to her, cocooned into her old friend's embrace.

"Everything is going to be OK, Jenny. I'm your evermore."

THE CONTRACT

There was nothing special about the day I died.

Everything was the same as it is always is. I woke up. I plodded downstairs to make a cup of coffee, feed the ungrateful cat, listen to the radio and think about the day ahead.

I like to think of myself as a smart guy. Of course I spend my days with the dregs of society, the lowlifes, the no morals scoundrels and anyone who operates outside of the law.

Edwin Burke would describe them as the swinish multitude" but still, of all the things that could happen to me while I earn a buck, dying never

figured in my plans.
I do my job, keep my mouth shut and I avoid any trouble. See no evil, hear no evil.
But today was different.
Some people have a hunch when things aren't going to go well. You spend your life living on your wits, you learn to listen to your instincts right?
Take the day some vermin left a car full of explosives next to mine. I had an inkling, let's call it suspicion, the vehicle wasn't supposed to be there. A quick call to the bomb squad proved me right - I watched safely from a distance as they blew the car up and took mine with it. Bits of me would be getting scraped off the tarmac if I'd been in there.
Then there was the time a scummy lowlife pulled out a knife threatening to slit me from ear to ear. That day I was prepared. A flimsy kitchen knife is no match for my faithful and ever present friend the bagh nakh - that's a tiger claw to you - I always keep it on my person since I spend my days dealing with hotheaded punks who think they're unbeatable

tough guys. He wasn't feeling so tough after I tore his face open and left his skin hanging in shreds.
I guess it comes with the territory. You see, I'm a 'gun for hire', maybe you would call me a hitman.
I'm not just any hitman though.
I don't do women or children.
The men I kill are miscreants and grifters.
I like to think I'm doing society a favour. I'm ridding them of the degenerates who've committed every crime you can think of.
It's a public service, really.
People like me mean people like you can sleep soundly in your bed at night.
And I was the best.
Of course there were always younger and fitter who thought they could beat me at my own game.
I don't mind admitting that I'm getting older, my bones are creaking and my movements aren't as fast as they used to be.
But I'm still the best in the business and so when death came I wasn't ready.

I'm getting ahead of myself. Like I said, it started off just like any other day - I had an early morning hit job. Get in and out, do the deed before the so called 'victim' even knew he was dying. Actually he'd be dead before he even managed to open his eyes.
I took a huge gulp of my coffee and poured the rest down the sink.
My wife was still asleep. She knew I worked for villains but she never asked any questions. It's one of the reasons I married her. She loved me enough to trust me. As long as I was home every night she didn't care. My job gave her a nice life. She didn't have to work. She spent her days shopping and preening herself. A lady who lunched. She's not the brightest but damn, she's good to look at. She's got the brains of an airhead. If it doesn't look good, she's not interested. The perfect wife for a contract killer.
If I'd known I was going to die that day I'd have climbed back into bed with her for one last 'tumble in the hay', to feel human and alive one last time.
But of course I had no idea the grim reaper was

coming so did nothing and left her in peaceful slumber as I departed the house in the pre-dawn darkness.

The chilly morning air clung to my skin and I shivered involuntarily. Birds were chirping away in the distance. The car was like a block of ice and while I waited for it to heat my thoughts turned to my wife again.

We'd met in a bar only three months before and married within four weeks. How cliched and foolish, I hear you say.

She managed to reel me in pretty quick. I'm a sucker for a red-head with green eyes and a cheeky grin.

I'm not a vain man but I know my looks and my height are a magnet for men and women. I'm what you might call 'wholesome looking', I'm over 6 foot tall, thick head of dark hair, green eyes and blessed with naturally white teeth.

I don't look like a serial killer which is what I guess I am.

The real me is easy going and friendly. I'm a fun-

loving, patient and kind guy.
I knew she was going to be someone special when she didn't fall my customary patter with the ladies. In fact, she told me to take a hike. It was at that moment I knew I'd found my equal, my soulmate. She was intimidating and arousing. Sure she's not exactly Einstein but she is my everything.
The rumbling of a train nearby jolted me out of my daydream. It was time to go. The job today wasn't just any old kill - this time it was personal.
I had received a call from an old friend, Jake. We had served time together in Afghanistan and had remained close ever since.
His wife had been attacked. It had been as vicious and brutal as it had been unexpected. They'd jumped her one night when she'd strayed into a rough area on a night out with friends. She was a tiny thing and no match for three burly men.
The ringleader was a local drug kingpin. Jake doesn't know what I do for a living so he'd come up with a plan for us to take them down together.

One last SNAFU for two battle-weary old Joes.
But I owed Jake.
He had saved my skin more than once out in the field.
I figured this was one score I could settle on his behalf.
I had met up with him a few days before at a rundown diner on the outskirts of town. He was sitting in a booth, nursing a cup of coffee with a thousand-yard stare. I slid into the seat across from him and ordered a black coffee.
"So, what's the plan?" I asked, leaning in.
Jake's eyes flicked up to meet mine. "We need to take down the main man. Then we go after the other two fuckers. They're heavily armed but I don't care."
"How is she?" My question had caught him off-guard. We weren't emotional types. We dealt with the practicalities of life and took whatever was thrown at us. Nobody ever asked if we were OK. His eyes flashed with anger then sadness.
"She's struggling, man. I can't get her to talk to me.

She is just a shell. Running on empty."

"I've got a stash of weapons and ammo back at my place. We'll need to gear up before we head out," he said.

It felt like old times except it wasn't. Jake had built a civilian life for himself. A good law-abiding life. I couldn't let him fuck it up. I killed for a living. I was good at it. In fact, it's about the only thing I am good at. Watching someone take their last breath doesn't faze me at all. Especially when they deserve it.

I made all the right noises as Jake plotted and planned his revenge but he couldn't know the only reason I'd met with him was to get information. I was going to take them all out myself. Less risk. In and out, quick kills.

Drug man lived in the suburbs. Figures someone like him would want to maintain that air of respectability. That's the thing with lowlifes - they think nobody knows, that their grubby way of life is a secret. They don't have the intelligence to realise you can practically smell the stench of delinquency. Adrenaline had kicked in. My stomach churned with anticipation. I put my hand in my pocket and felt the cold steel of my tiger claw. It comforted me as I approached the back door of the bungalow that was in darkness. I had already studied the layout online. The back door led to the kitchen and from there it was a left to the hallway and upstairs. I figured drug man would sleep in the largest bedroom which, handily, was adjacent to the top of the stairs. He'd never hear me coming.

Some people say right before they die their life flashes before their eyes.

What.A.Crock.

As I reached the top of the stairs, my breathing suddenly felt laboured. My heart was racing. I could feel my tongue and throat begin to swell. I put my hand on the wall and tried to get some air into my lungs. I made it onto the landing and staggered around. I felt my head swell.

Then came the second wave. I knew I was going to die. I had time to only think of the irony before death claimed me - the target was surviving this day.

Jake held out his hands. Her eyes were red and puffy from crying so much. She grabbed his hands and he was surprised by the strength in them. "I'm so sorry. I just can't believe it, he was super fit." Jake said.
She didn't say anything but gave a slight shrug of her shoulders.
He continued speaking: "If you need anything at all, give me a call. I know we don't know each other very well but I know he'd want me to look out for you."
She smiled but it didn't reach her eyes.
"Thank-you Jake." She replied and guided him to the open front door.
"If you don't mind, I'm going to lie down now. We've, I mean, I've, had a lot of visitors today." She smiled again.
Jake knew he was being ushered out. He gave her

another hug and took his leave.

She closed the door and leant against it. Finally the house was silent.

She walked up to their bedroom and lay on the bed.

Memories of him raced into her mind. Their long walks on the beach, the way he held her hand and grabbed her for a long kiss when they were out in public, the sound of his laugh. His touch. And his allergy to penicillin.

She was surprised when she felt a tear escape the corner of her eye and roll down her cheek.

Her mobile rang. She saw the name on the screen and sighed.

"Is it done?" The caller asked.

"Yes," she said.

"Payment will be made by the usual method." He said and hung up the phone.

She swept her hand across her wet cheek and shook her head.

This wasn't the moment for emotions.

It was time for her next job.

THE DARKEST DAY

Life, thought Emily Harris, just wants to come along and punch you right in the gut when you least expect it. Her husband had decided this morning was a good time to tell her he was leaving her.

Again.

She'd been glueing on her false eyelashes when he suddenly announced he was moving in with a "mate."

He'd called her Ems. She heard the whine in his tone. Always the victim.

“Ems, I need some space. I’ve arranged to stay with a mate for a bit. It’s only temporary like. You know my mental health hasn't been great lately."

Now she was stuck in a traffic jam and already over an hour late for work.

Her chest felt tight. A heart attack would sum up this day already, she thought.

Emily looked in the rearview mirror and winced at her red eyes. Why she was wasting precious tears was beyond her. Martin had only been back six months and she'd known after their last separation it was only a matter of time before he was off again. Could any man resist a younger, prettier woman untouched by the ravages of childbirth, menopause and too many maltesers?

Martin Harris liked his women stick thin and seductive, not slightly rounded and permanently exhausted.

'You need to give your head a wobble. There's no fool like an old fool and that's you Emily Harris. 50 years on this planet and you still haven't learnt that the only person you can count on is yourself.' She spoke out loud to herself.

It didn't take a genius to work out the 'mate' in this case is his new girlfriend. It won't last - he'll be turfed out on his ear when she realises he's still got to pay the mortgage and upkeep for his child.
Eventually the designer handbags and romantic dinners will stop and the woman will send him packing. He'll come crawling back with his tail between his legs begging for forgiveness and like an even bigger idiot you'll let him because you're scared of being old and alone,' she sighed.
A horn beeping from behind startled her out of her self-scolding and she lifted a hand as if in apology to the van driver before putting the car into gear and inching forward the three yards the traffic in front had moved.
"Wanker," she muttered under her breath. "Not as if we're moving anywhere fast," she added.
She noticed he was right up against her back bumper which annoyed her. "For heavens sakes, is there any need?" She turned to her right and saw the traffic was moving a little faster on that side so when the

next space opened up she drifted over and slotted in perfectly.

For a moment she felt a little smug. The van driver was still stuck in the slow lane about half a dozen cars behind her while she was moving steadily. "Bloody white van men, think they own the damn road." She sighed again.

Today was tough enough without adding road rage into the mix. She was still a good 10 miles from the office; she should have called in sick. But with Martin moving out she knows from past experience she won't see a penny from him so she can't afford to lose her job now.

Her thoughts turned to her daughter. Emily felt sad that when Martin made his big announcement, Christina didn't even look up from her phone. The father-daughter relationship just wasn't there. Martin had spent so many years flitting in and out that his presence or absence didn't register with their daughter. He had never been hands-on and if truth be told he resented the child somewhat -

her existence meant less money for him and being forced to endure family things she knew bored him. He'd rather be in the pub or with his latest girlfriend than helping Christina with homework or, God forbid, a trip to the local zoo. A pang of guilt flashed through Emily. Life would've been so much easier for them if she'd only had the backbone to kick Martin to the kerb when Christina was a baby and he cheated for the first time.

But no family around meant Martin, as inept as he was, was her only support blanket. She knew she was pathetic and hated herself for that co-dependency. She'd spent most of Christina's life putting their needs on the back burner and letting Martin trample all over them.

A flash of white out the passenger window caused her to turn. White van man had caught up with her and was staring intently into her car. She didn't know him but he looked so furious she instinctively recoiled and kept her eyes straight ahead. Tension in her shoulders told her she was gripping the steering wheel tightly. The white van was dangerously close to her side of the road. Anger bubbled to the surface. She'd had enough of shitty men and their behaviour. She rolled down the window. "Oi asshole, stick to your own side of the road or hand your driving licence back to the circus!" To her surprise he didn't scream back at her but instead a sardonic smile crossed his face. He was quite handsome she noticed. But he had a cold look about him that gave her the shivers.

As if by magic the traffic jam suddenly cleared. Emily put her foot down and sped away from the van feeling unnerved by his overblown reaction. She still didn't know what she'd done wrong when he tooted her but whatever it was didn't deserve his fury. He was looking at her like he knew her and despised her intensely. An odd feeling really. She'd had run-ins before on the road, the odd 'get it up ye' and 'you get your licence in a lucky bag' squabble with random drivers over the years but this felt more personal.

She pulled into the office carpark and gave herself a mental shake. Time for work and salvage something from this day.

The carpark was empty when Emily left her office at 7pm. 500 people worked in her office block and everyone had scarpered early. It was Friday and she had stayed back late because she'd been so late this morning.

She'd called Christina earlier and told her to order some pizza for tea and she'd be home by 7.30 so they could chill out on the sofa, eat pizza and binge on mindless television.

Emily knew Christina wouldn't mention her dad. She didn't care enough about him to worry about him deserting the family home.

The sad fact of the matter was Christina preferred it to be just the two of them. Emily adjusted the strap of her handbag on her shoulder and rooted around for her keys. She could hear the low hum of distant traffic but the estate was deserted, everyone had packed up and gone home for the weekend. There was a soft glow from the street lighting; the shadows on the road made it seem like it was stretching on forever. She wished she'd parked a little closer to the building. She looked back and could just make out the outline of the night security guard sitting at reception. Maybe she should go and ask if he'll escort her to her car which she reckoned was still a couple of hundred yards away.

"You are your own worst enemy. You have walked this car park a million times and you've never been scared. What is wrong with you woman?" She tutted at herself and wobbled her head as if to shake off her paranoia.

She knew her imagination was in overdrive. She'd felt unsettled all day, first because of Martin then the van driver. She couldn't forget the way he'd looked at her. It was the same resentful look Christina gave her whenever she said 'no' to something. She wrapped her fingers around her car keys and vaguely remembered something about clasping the key in between your knuckles in case of an attack. Poke them right in the eye.

"Yeah that makes sense if you can keep your cool long enough while you're being dragged and manhandled by someone bigger and stronger," she thought.

She was just reaching her car when her pocket vibrated. Unknown caller.

"Hello?"

Silence.

"Helllo?" Still the line was silent.

She was about to hang up when she heard the person breathing.

"Hey. Who is this?" She heard background noise and strained to hear. There was a familiar sound on the line. Christina!

She could hear her daughter singing along to a song.

"Christina? If this is one of your daft pranks it isn't funny. I'm on my way home now!" The caller was still silently breathing down the line and Christina shouted "Alexa, play Beyonce," seemingly oblivious to the phone scenario.

The line went dead.

Emily started to dial Christina's number when the screen lit up again with another call.

Her friend Alison. "Hey Ali. Can I call you back in a minute? I've just had a strange call from Christina."

The line was silent. "Al?" Nothing. No response.

"What the fuck is going on Alison?" The phone went black.

Emily's heart was hammering as she got into her car and locked the doors. She tried to call Christina back but there was no answer. The house phone rang out too.

"Tonight is not the night for playing jokes on me," she raged. Her call to Alison went unanswered. Her daughter's phone went straight to answer phone. It was switched off.

Emily fumed. 'Just you wait, Christina Harris, we'll see how amusing you find it when I confiscate your bloody phone!'

Steadying her breathing, Emily fiddled with her car's stereo system and found a radio station playing classical music. That'll do, she thought. I need something to calm me down, find some zen. What an unbelievably shitty day.
She pulled out of the carpark and onto the main road. She felt strangely relieved when she noticed how busy the road was. Traffic and people going about their lives. For the last few hours she'd felt alone in the world which was a ridiculous thought but she was self-aware enough to know her emotions were all over the place today.
Thanks to her crappy husband. She knew she needed to work on her own self-esteem and her relationship with her daughter. It didn't take a genius to work out she allowed Martin to mistreat her so badly because she was low on confidence.
Calm descended on her. Martin wasn't worth the tears or trauma he brought into their lives. He was just a man. A very ordinary one at that.
As she drove, Emily found herself lost in thought,

contemplating all the ways she could take control of her life.

She could maybe even find a new job and a new house. A completely new start for her and Christina.

As she approached a stop light, she heard a sudden screech of brakes and the sound of metal crunching. Emily's car shook from the impact. She looked in the rearview mirror and saw a white van had collided with her.

No! Surely not?, she thought. It had to be co-incidence. She unbuckled her seat belt and stepped out of the car and was about to walk to the van when she recognised the driver.

It was white van man from earlier!

Anger and fear surged through her. "What the hell?" she muttered.

Her heart was hammering. The driver was smoking a cigarette and gazing at her. He didn't move. Emily was rooted to the spot. For a second she didn't know what to do. Should she confront him or get back in her car. She looked around and the street was

deserted. There was nobody about.
She felt scared. She jumped back into her car and locked the doors.
This man was following her, she was sure of it. Assessing any damage to her car can wait, she thought. She needed to get away from him. She pushed her foot down hard on the accelerator and sped away.
She almost lost control when her phone sparked into life, the ringtone coming through the car speakers as the robotic voice droned: 'Alison calling'...Emily hesitated before answering the call, wondering if it was safe to take it. But she couldn't ignore it either. The earlier calls had freaked Emily out. What if something was wrong with Allison and she was calling for help? She took a deep breath and answered, putting the call on speaker mode.
"Alison? Are you okay?" she asked.
There was no answer, only the sound of heavy breathing on the other end. Emily's heart started racing again. She didn't like where this was going.

"Alison, please answer me. Are you--"
The call ended abruptly, leaving Emily in a state of panic. She tried calling back, but the line was dead.
Something was seriously wrong. She felt like she was being watched, like there was someone following her every move.
She needed to get home and make sure Christina was OK. Then she'd deal with Alison.
Emily drove as fast as she could, weaving in and out of traffic, going through red lights. She knew she was acting like a madwoman but her only thoughts were for her daughter.
'Alison calling...' chimed the car again. Emily hit answer on reflex. Relief coursed through her at the sound of her best friend's voice. "Emily! Don't go home...They're...." the call cut off.
Her stomach dropped. Emily's hands tightened on the steering wheel as she tried to make sense of what Alison was saying. "Don't go home? Who are 'they'?" she muttered to herself. Her mind racing with possibilities.

This wasn't a prank. She should call the police. And say what? My daughter pocket dialled me, a van hit my car and my best friend has called me with a warning not to go home. They'll think I'm a madwoman.

A tiny part of her still believed Alison and Christina had set this up as some kind of joke.

She pulled into her street. The house was in darkness. Usually when Christina was home alone, every light in the house was on.

All thoughts of her own safety disappeared from her mind as she sprinted from the car to her front door.

She fumbled with her keys and unlocked the door.

As she stepped inside, she could hear a strange noise coming from upstairs. She tiptoed up the stairs, her heart in her throat.

With each step she took, the sound, like someone crying, was getting louder.

Her bedroom door was slightly open. Slowly she walked towards it, trying to stay as quiet as she possibly could.

There was a whimper and a moan so she pushed the door open and stepped inside.
The room was in darkness but she could make out the shape of a figure lying on the bed.
Mother's instinct pushed her to rush forward then she hesitated. Her eyes had adjusted to the dark and in a millisecond she could tell whoever it was in the bed, it wasn't her daughter.
Heart pounding she crept closer and reached for the lamp on the bedside table. The figure groaned. It was a woman. Emily felt a surge of anger amidst the fear. Who the hell was this person lying in her bed? And where was Christina. Emily lifted the lamp over her head and was about to strike when the woman groaned again and shifted in the bed.
'Stop!" the woman croaked, holding up her arms in defence. "It's me, it's Alison!"
Alison's face was distorted. A bloody pulpy mess.
Emily staggered back, the lamp slipping from her hand and crashing to the floor. Fear and confusion was making her head spin.

Alison was groaning and telling Emily to run. Her breathing was raspy. She was seriously hurt but she was still trying to speak through her injuries. Emily dropped to her knees and held her friend.
She felt in her pocket for her mobile but realised in her rush to get inside she'd left it in the car.
"Alison, don't try to speak. I'm just going downstairs to use the phone and call for help. I'll be back in two minutes." Alison was shaking her head frantically. Emily could see the panic in the tiny slits of her eyes. "It's not safe," Alison managed to whisper. "Run, Emily. They're still here."
Emily's heart rate spiked again. "Who's still here? What happened to you?" She asked urgently.
Her mind was racing. Who could have done this to Alison? She felt a creeping sense of dread as she thought about her daughter, alone and vulnerable.
"Christina.."Alison croaked. She tried to sit up.
"Don't move Alison. I'm going to get help."
She stood up and took a deep breath. She needed to think fast and stay focused. As she hurried out of the

room, her mind raced through different scenarios that could have led to Alison's injuries. Had she disturbed an intruder? Was someone breaking in when Alison came into the house? Where was her daughter? Was she lying injured in another room? She was certain that whoever had done this was still in the house, waiting for her to make a move.

Emily pushed aside her worries and crept out into the dark hall, her heart pounding with every step. She needed to get help, find her daughter and get out of there before it was too late.

She broke into a run down the stairs and out the front door to her car, fumbling for her keys. She could feel the sweat on her palms as she unlocked the door and grabbed her phone from the passenger seat. As she dialled 999 she looked up to Christina's bedroom window and thought she saw a shadow. For a second she considered staying outside until the police came. She needed to get to her daughter.

The operator asked what emergency service she wanted.

“Police and an ambulance please. Hurry! I have an intruder and my friend is injured.” The operator asked for her address and asked if she was safe. “Yes, I’m outside but I’m going back in.” “Ma’am, I’d urge you to stay outside until the officers arrive.” Emily hung up and ran to the boot. Martin had insisted she keep tools in her car and amongst that was a nut wrench. She grabbed it and ran back into the house.
A figure was bent over Alison. “Hey!” Emily shouted. The figure straightened up and turned around. “Mum!” “Christina!” Emily was across the room in two strides and enveloped her daughter in a huge hug. “My God Christina. I thought something had happened to you.” Christina looked as if she’d been crying. “Oh mum! I had to hide!”
Alison was drifting in and out of consciousness. She could hear the voices of Emily and Christina. She desperately tried to stay awake long enough to warn her friend but she kept blacking out. Just before darkness claimed her again she heard Christina say: “Mum, did you call the police?” It felt like hours had

passed but it was only seconds.
"Emily…" Alison wheezed. Emily knelt down at the side of the bed and dropped the nut wrench. She didn't realise she was still holding onto it. She grabbed Alison's hand. "Help is on the way Ali. Just hang tight. Don't try to speak."
Alison was shaking her head and was trying to sit up. "It was…"
Christina grabbed Alison's other hand. "Oh Aunty Alison don't talk. The police are on their way and so is an ambulance." Somehow Alison had the strength to pull her hand away and made a growling sound at the back of her throat.
Emily was confused. She'd been friends with Alison for over 40 years, through thick and thin. She was Christina's Godmother. Christina's eyes had narrowed. She looked angry. Emily felt rather than heard soft footsteps behind her and in that split second she saw the fear flash across Alison's face.
She was pulled to her feet by arms around her neck. "You stupid stupid bitch!," screamed Christina who

punched Alison's head as she scrambled to her feet and rounded on her mother. "Why couldn't you have just fucking crashed your car today?" Emily couldn't speak but horror dawned on her. Christina had done this to Alison.

"Look what you made me do to Alison? This is all your fault!" She slapped her mother across the face.

"Let her go, stupid…" she said to the figure holding Emily. His grip relaxed. Emily was too stunned to do anything. She didn't even feel the sting on her cheek from Christina's slap.

Confusion reigned. "Christina? Wha.."

"Just fucking shut up Mum. God your voice! It drives me insane. I need to think!" Christina knew the police would be there any second. Her eyes fell on the nut wrench.

"Babe, pick that up…." the figure behind her moved into Emily's line of vision. It was white van man.

"You!" Emily shouted.

Christina giggled. She was actually laughing. "For once I'm actually happy to see your stupid face stumped. This is my boyfriend. If he'd done his job right earlier today you would've crashed your car and all of this could have been avoided! But no you had to go through the city to work instead of the back roads. No chance of running you off the road there!"

Now it made sense why he looked so angry this morning. She'd scuppered their plans. Van man was meant to run her off the road and make it look like an accident; she wasn't sure how Alison had been caught up in this.

She had to keep them distracted for a few more minutes. She was frightened they were going to batter Alison with the wrench and finish her off before doing whatever with her. Surely the police couldn't be much longer now. She reckoned it was almost ten minutes since she'd called them.

Emily just wanted to weep. What had happened to her beautiful, sweet little girl? She didn't recognise this person standing in front of her, anger and bitterness seeping out of every pore. "Christina, I

don't understand…"
Christina's face was screwed up. "Don't you get it? I hate you Mum. I have done for years. Your stupid bending over backwards and letting Dad use and abuse you. You have no spine, no backbone! You let him treat you like a dog but then you turn around and try and lay down the law with me. You want to be involved in every aspect of my life but you won't do anything about your own! I've wanted rid of you for years. It should just be dad and me!"
"You're 15! And him? How old is he? 30?!" Van man stayed silent.
"This is why you have to die! You're more concerned with his age than you are about the fact your best friend is dying and your daughter sent someone to run you off the road! You can't help yourself! I can't fucking breathe when you're around. You're obsessed with me! I'm not your best pal! I begged Dad to leave you and take me with him. I actually introduced him to his latest girlfriend! He's been trying to be good because he felt sorry for you! He

comes back to you out of pity, it's so pathetic. I knew you'd never approve of Lee so I made sure Dad had a girlfriend and when he was leaving I was going with him but the stupid idiot refused to take me!"
She laughed incredulously. "He's so self-centred that I can do what I like when he's about but not you."
She made a whining voice "Oh Christina it's late you should get to bed, Oh Christina you don't need make up, Christina, let's have a movie night...Christina, Christina, Christina....I'm all you think about!"
Tears flowed down Emily's cheeks. "You're my child..."
Emily didn't see the wrench come down on her head. She was dead before she hit the ground.

Christina wiped away her tears. She slipped her arm through Martin's as they stood in line greeting the mourners. "It'll all be over soon, Dad."
Christina kept her head down and let her hair cover her face as she smiled to herself thinking of the last

few weeks. She felt a sudden rush of euphoria when she thought back to the headlines in all the national newspapers.

'Teenage daughter finds mum and best friend slain in house of horrors bloodbath.'

AFTERWORD

I hope you enjoyed this short foray into my dark imagination.
Look out for my debut novel, Death Knock, which will be published in March 2024.
Angie Ferguson is a fearless reporter for a Scottish national newspaper.
She's on the hunt for a missing teenager from a tough Edinburgh housing estate. The police don't seem to care and her desperate parents have no-one to turn to except Angie.
Isla Montgomery might be from the wrong side of the tracks but she's a model student with a heart of gold and a bright future ahead.
When Isla's boyfriend, the son of Scotland's Justice Minister, turns up dead from an apparent suicide,

she sets out to prove he murdered Isla.
Angie thinks it's an open and shut case. But is it? Where is Isla and what secrets led to her disappearance?
Angie is warned off the case by her best friend, Detective Inspector Grace Avery, who is heading up a secret investigation.
The two women are on a collision course that will test their friendship to the limit and rock the Scottish Political establishment to the core.

ACKNOWLEDGEMENT

There are a few people who I need to mention for their help and advice, particularly when I was full of doubts about writing fiction never mind publishing a book.

Ruth M, I can see you rolling your eyes and wondering what I'm pulling you into now. Your friendship, loyalty and support means everything to me. You're a star, dolly.

Douglas S, you answer my questions, you're always helpful and polite and you always have words of encouragement - even when you're on writing deadlines yourself. Thank you for being kind and supportive in all my writing endeavours.

Jen H, you read early versions of these stories and offered motivation at a time I needed it most. You're my bonus daughter and I'm very lucky to have you in my life.

John W, a simple thank you for being supportive,

helpful and encouraging.
Sandra M, my wee buddy. You read everything I write and always say you love it and can't wait for the next one. How lucky am I to have such an amazing pal who rallys me to get writing?
Nick S, your confidence in me is something to cherish. I'm very lucky to have you in my life. Regardless of what happens with our project, I just know we will always be friends.
Leanne & Kevin - the ones who everything was for. I hope you're both as proud of me as I am you.
My mum who loves to read and says the stories in this book are "very good" - that's praise indeed.
My wee bro: you're a constant pain in the botty but you've always got my back.
D, what can I say I haven't already? You shoulder the burdens and give me space and encouragement to be creative. You are my person and I don't know what I'd do without you.

ABOUT THE AUTHOR

JD Hamilton is a professional writer. She lives in Scotland.

Printed in Great Britain
by Amazon